Midnight Sun

JC Alva

Published by JC Alva, 2023.

MIDNIGHT SUN

First edition. January 7, 2023.

Copyright © 2023 JC Alva.

ISBN: 979-8215732342

Written by JC Alva.

Table of Contents

To my wife Rosanna,

May you always be the fire that brightens my dark cold days.

Midnight Sun
By
JC Alva

In a small cold Russian town, on the outskirts of Khabarovsk, 30 kilometers from the Chinese border, a Russian police patrol car comes to a gas station to refill its tanks just before 2 pm in the afternoon.

There were two small boys playing soccer on the empty street in front of the station. The patrol car stops under the half-lit flickering lights of the station and two police officers come out of their vehicle almost at the same time.

While one of the police officers was punching in the buttons to activate the automatic refilling machine, he yells at the two small boys to be careful while playing on the street.

The other officer heads straight to the station's convenience store where an elderly man in thick glasses, wearing an old worn-out brown sweater and scarf, was at the cashier reading an old, Russian edition of Time magazine.

There was traditional Russian folk music playing in the background while the police officer waved at the old man as he passes him on his way to the sausage warmers that were slowly spinning inside a cylindrical glass console. The officer presses some buttons and the sausage machine starts making two sandwiches.

The officer goes to the next lane to grab some snacks and opens a refrigerated glass cabinet and takes canned energy drinks from its shelves. He returns to the sausage machine to see that the machine has already prepared two sausage sandwiches, smoking warm, wrapped in individual cardboard trays.

He carries some of the snacks by his teeth so he could pick up the two prepared sandwiches. He goes to the old man at the cashier and puts down the items in front of the cashier. The old man puts down his magazine and asks in Russian

"Is that all?"

The old man starts passing the items through his scanner and starts putting all the items in a shopping bag. The officer pulls out a card and swipes it on the cashier's sensor. The machine prints out a receipt and the old man tears it and drops it into the shopping bag.

"Have a good day officer..."

Says the old man as he grabs his old magazine and resumes his leisurely reading.

As the officer steps out of the store and into the cold to join the other police officer watching the machine finish refueling their patrol car, they suddenly hear a roaring sound from the sky.

Suddenly, bursting out of the cloudy skies were two Military Transport Carriers. The huge crafts had long semi-cylindrical bodies and had two pairs of forward and rear thrusters that swiveled independently to stabilize the craft to a hover, and large forward and rear gun turrets extending out of the craft.

The police officer nearest the patrol car instinctively grabbed his assault rifle from the rear seats and started to look for heavy cover behind the concrete pillars of the station.

The second police officer sets down the shopping bag on top of the refilling machine. He pulls out his pistol from his thigh holster and runs to the left of the hovering craft to see its markings.

As the craft makes a slow turn, the police officer can see a Red Star in front of a Red Band, with a Chinese character in the middle of the star. He shouts

"Chinese Troop Carrier!"

as his partner cocks his weapon. The old man from the convenience store walks out with an old hunter's shotgun.

More people started coming out of the small buildings and homes just across the station.

A few cars also stopped to see what was going on. The wind from the thrusters of the huge carriers was blinding the two officers as they would begin yelling to everyone to clear the area.

The people were too curious to listen to the officers, and more of them started coming out to see what has awakened their sleepy town.

The two small boys playing soccer were staring up at the Chinese carrier, not noticing that their soccer ball was being blown down the road by the winds from the thrusters. The mother of one of the small boys came running down the street calling out his son's name.

The two boys were almost directly under the hovering craft as the screaming mother was frantically rushing toward her son. The old man starts walking slowly, aiming for the carrier and the police officer yells at him not to shoot. The old man trips on a loose brick on the pavement and the hair-trigger-sensitive shotgun goes off.

The carriers start firing all their guns in all directions as the second carrier hovered further down the street and started firing at anything that moved. Its huge caliber guns would tear into the concrete walls of the buildings and slice through the flesh of all the people on the street.

The police with the assault rifles returned fire, but the heavily armored carrier deflected the rifle's bullets. The mother running for her child was hit on her thigh, almost severing her leg from her body. Her son sees his mother down on the street bleeding and starts running towards her. The police officer sees the child running towards the rapid fire of the carrier. He runs across the street and grabs the child and heads straight for a narrow alley safe from incoming fire. He hides the child inside a thick metal garbage dumpster.

Amid the noise of the continuous gunfire, He shouts at the little boy not to move from where he was, then he looks out at the street to see the other boy's lifeless body not far from where the soccer ball rested on the street.

He could see his partner firing at the craft only to get hit as his concrete cover is obliterated by the rapid heavy fire from the gunship.

He could still hear the cries of the wounded mother on the street as he sees the cars shredded to ribbons and dead bodies scattered everywhere. What was once clear clean streets was now a torn-up concrete battle zone with dead bodies everywhere.

The carrier stopped firing and the only sound was from the huge thrusters of the hovering craft, that started to descend to the street.

The carrier landed and a rear bay door started opening. Out came unmarked soldiers in all black with bonnets to cover their faces. They were followed by five Chinese soldiers in uniform, all tied bound from behind.

The police officer can see soldiers in black bring each captive Chinese soldier to different corners of the street. Then, one by one, the Chinese soldiers were executed, their hands were untied, and the soldiers in black dropped Chinese-made weapons beside the bodies, making it seem like the Chinese soldiers were the ones in the firefight.

As the police officer started to crawl back to the alley, He hears a woman's voice say in Russian,

"Where are you going?"

He turns to see a woman, straight long black hair, Asian looking, with a soldier beside her pointing a rifle at him. He puts up his hands to surrender. Then the woman pulls out a pistol from under her jacket and says:

"Sorry, not this time..."

She fires straight into his temple and his body falls lifeless in the narrow alley. The woman gives orders to the men and they all head back into the carrier. She was the last to step into the carrier as she stares at the carnage of her work.

Two days later, at Zebra Station, Military Outpost, Antarctica. The room was dark, except for tiny lights that gave soft ambient lighting to the room when John was awakened by the high-pitched beeping sound of his bedside alarm clock.

He squints as he slowly opens his eyes to focus on the digital alarm clock's face. He slowly crawls out of his thick military green blanket and reaches one arm toward his bedside alarm clock. His neat laser art of a marine tattoo, skull and two crisscross knives behind it was visible on his arm. He finally reaches it and gives it a light tap. The sound of the alarm stops. He starts trying to hold his breath so that his brain would be deoxygenated from his deep sleep.

He pushes the rest of the thick blanket off himself as the slowly gets to a sitting position at the edge of his bed. He yawns and stretches his arms out. He then arches his chest forward and pushes himself off the bed. He slowly walks towards a dark-tinted window and taps its surface. A woman's voice came from the surround speakers in the room

"Window set to clear..."

The windows black tint started to vanish as the natural light from outside would start brightening the room. John would scratch his eyes and tries to focus on the view of this window. A vast white ice landscape. John then walks towards his bathroom and proceeds with his morning rituals.

He turns on a monitor on his kitchen counter to view his satellite feed news. As he takes a sip from his coffee cup, he hears news of encounters between Russian and Chinese forces.

The reports said that a Russian village near the border of both countries was attacked by the Chinese Liberation Army. Chinese news media claims that the Russians were spreading fake news, and were just making excuses for their attacks on Chinese border forces.

A pleasant chime rang out and John walked towards the compact food processing machine to grab his daily Eggs, Toast, and Bacon breakfast steaming, as he brought the plate up to his nose and sat at the

kitchen counter without taking his eyes off the reporter on his monitor. As he started eating his breakfast using a Spork, a combination of a Spoon and Fork, on one hand, the radio that was sitting on its charging base came alive with a woman's voice.

"This is Ice Rover 211 calling Zebra Station, John, are you there? Come in Please..."

With bacon and eggs still in his mouth, he takes a quick sip of his coffee to clear his throat and grabs the radio off its base.

"This is Zebra Station to Rover 211, Good morning, Debra. You're out early today, aren't you?"

John walks to the high window and grabs the binoculars with his other hand still on the radio and started looking for Debra through his binoculars.

"I'm not early John. You're just late..."

John smiles as he sees the bright red ice rover plowing through the thick snow toward him.

"How about some bacon and eggs? You know I make the meanest coffee this side of Antarctica..."

Debra starts laughing on the radio.

"With minus fifteen decrees, any coffee will do...Besides, I always know what happens after coffee John..."

John smiles and puts down his binoculars and says:

"My bed is still warm Debra"

Debra starts laughing again.

"Breakfast first, Coffee, then let's talk about your bed..."

John starts pushing some buttons on the food processor and starts clearing some of his unwashed dishes into the automatic dishwashing machine.

"Just come in Debra. Breakfast will be ready when you get in." John suddenly hears a news flash saying that a United States Satellite has been hit by another unidentified satellite and will re-enter Earth's atmosphere in 3 Hours and is expected to land somewhere in the Antarctic region, while keeping his eyes on the monitor, he radios back to Debra.

"I'll just check Davis Station if they have any updates for me. Your breakfast will be ready for you here in my kitchen."

John starts walking to his communications area to check on updates. He sits on his command module and opens a digital map of a wide area of Antarctica projected on a large glass pane. He goes to the glass pane and with the tips of his fingers, rotates the image to widen the digital map.

"Map, show satellite tracking on sectors D to F, South 7 Degrees..."

The computer answers in a soft motherly voice

"Computing for given sectors"

The image started changing, zooming in on John's given sectors. The large monitor showed the Real-time movements of the satellites on the screen.

"Map, Include sector G and time-lapse to minus 3 hours..."

The large monitor momentarily froze and started once more computing showing the movements of the satellites 3 hours ago. John had noticed a satellite whose trajectory been had altered.

He zooms in on the particular satellite and taps on its image

"Identify satellite..."

The computer divided the large glass monitor in half. The left half still shows the given sectors, while the right half was generating a comprehensive diagram and schematics of the satellite.

"Satellite identified as Helios V, a U.S. geostationary satellite that monitors the southern boundary of Russia and the Northern boundary of China. Launched in 2027, its main purpose was to monitor and detect military movement between the two countries as a result of the China-Indian Boarder War of 2026."

John taps on his keyboard to print out a hard copy of the Helios V.

"Compute for a new trajectory of Helios V"

The computer suddenly shows a wide view of the Antarctic map showing the trajectory of the satellite's re-entry to Earth. Then the computer says

"Helios V is scheduled to land on Sector F, Coordinates -74.962666 and 88.105458 South in two hours 37 minutes"

John enters the coordinates in his wristwatch and grabs the hard copy of the Helios V satellite. He runs back to his main quarters where he sees Debra sitting comfortably on one of the kitchen stools eating her breakfast and watching the news. Her cheeks were pinkish from the cold, light brown hair to her shoulders and the darkest of black eyes anyone has seen. The snow on her shoulders was just starting to melt on her bright red thick jacket and her grey fox fur scarf was just hanging on the backrest of another chair in the kitchen.

"Hi, John! Thanks for the breakfast. You know you should really learn to open the front door for a lady...especially if she comes bearing gifts..."

John walks to Debra and gives her a hug from behind.

"I miss you..." Debra licks her spork and turns her head to John giving him a quick smack to the lips.

"Miss me...I was just here the other day..."

John puts both his arms around her and holds her tighter from behind as he starts smelling her shiny hair and kissing her neck." Debra notices the printout that John was holding.

"What's that? A love letter?"

John releases her and grabs the stool beside her.

"Helios V,"

John says as he shows Debra the satellite schematics.

"Just before you came in, there was a news report that one of our satellites was attacked by another unidentified satellite. I was able to track which of our satellites got hit and where it's supposed to crash in the next two hours."

Debra starts taking off her thick red jacket showing off her slim but curvy body under a white body-hugging material that had small heating tubes running up from her back, to her shoulders, and down her arms.

She grabs the schematics from John. She starts studying the Schematics and runs her perfectly manicured slim fingers through the diagram.

"This satellite has a special heat shield that can protect the satellite's main components from re-entry damage. This is a military-built spy satellite. Really bulletproof."

As Debra continues to study the printout, John grabs Debra's coffee and takes a sip out of her lipstick-marked white cup.

"I know where it's falling..."

Says, John. Debra lays the schematic down on the kitchen counter and pulls John closer to her by grabbing the back of his neck.

"What about my after-breakfast delight?"

says Debra, as she starts kissing John. He responds by picking her up wildly and bringing her to his bedroom while Debra starts laughing.

The winds were starting to slow down when both John and Debra came out of the station that had stilts to keep the living quarters above the surface of the snow.

They head towards a covered garage to John's snow crawler that had camo white printed on its surface. It's a larger snow crawler, military-grade, had a higher clearance off the snow and had wider tracks. Its roof had twin large caliber automatic tracking guns and a flare system for anti-heat seeking missiles from above.

They both enter the crawler and John starts flicking on switches to start the vehicle. Debra, holding the printed-out schematics says

"Are you sure about the projected crash location?" John presses a large red start button, and the crawler came alive with the engine's noise and the vibration inside the vehicle.

"Sure, I'm Sure!"

John presses another green button and a woman's voice came through the speakers

"Opening Shelter Door"

The door in front of them starts lifting slowly as the bright light from the sun reflected off the snow was getting brighter. They both start putting on their sunglasses to relieve themselves of the snow's brightness. The crawler starts moving out of its shelter as it made deep tracks on the snow. They pass Debra's red snow crawler parked just beside the entrance of the station.

"You really need to request to get a newer crawler..."

says John. Debra rolls the schematics in her hands turning it into a stiff tube and hits John on the head.

"Spitfire! My crawler's name is Spitfire!"

Says Debra.

"She may be old but Spitfire has gotten me out of the most difficult situations..."

John takes a look at Debra, seeing that she was very sensitive about her crawler...

"Sorry Deb, didn't know you were in love with another..."

Debra grabs the keyboard that is connected by a swivel arm and attached to the console of the vehicle in front of her and starts punching in the coordinates that John had earlier downloaded. A 10-inch screen turns on the dash of the crawler and a waypoint is displayed.

"Waypoint on Screen, 132 kilometers to destination"

Debra then checks on the heating controls of the vehicle. She starts adjusting the heating controls "Your settings are too cold..." John swivels his head and takes a quick look at his temperature settings

"Looks just fine to me..."

Debra pulls back the end of the sleeve of her red jacket at her left wrist to expose her inner white suit heating linings.

"I better increase my temp then..."

As the crawler was plowing through the thick snow, a warning came up on the directional screen on the dashboard.

"Warning! Crevasse. Alternative waypoints as needed."

"Can Spitfire give you crevasse warnings?" John says with a smile.

Debra answers "...And when that system fails, what shall you do? Don't need it. I know where the dangerous ones are and where we can pass." As they near their waypoint, Debra sees black smoke on the horizon in front of them. She grabs binoculars from the vehicle's forward storage compartment, removes her sunglasses, and steadies herself from the vehicle's movements.

"See it? Asks John.

"Yup! There it is, just as your computer predicted, only about half a mile or so off."

As they get closer to the crash site, they could see the partially charred satellite that made a long skid mark as it plowed deeper into the snow where it came to a halt.

The smoke had lessened by the time they got out of their vehicle about 25 meters from the crash site. The cold wind started blowing harder, making it even more difficult for them to walk in the knee-deep soft snow.

Their cold headgear had a built-in camera that could record both stills and video streaming. Debra reaches for a switch just above her right ear area and turns on the camera as she walks closer to the charred satellite. John goes further down the parted snow area where the satellite first started plowing through the snow.

"I'm gonna go further down to see if anything else came off the satellite," John says.

The remains of the satellite were as big as a small car. Debra kneels down and clears some snow off the satellite to have a better view. She then grabs a palm full of snow to wash off a burnt part of the satellite.

She starts rubbing the satellite's surface with her gloved hands exposing a small access opening. She reaches for her thigh pocket and brings out a compact electric screwdriver. She first uses the tip of the screwdriver to clear the carbon buildup on the embedded screw heads, then starts removing the screws.

With the screws removed, she then tries to pry open the satellite's cover. She knocks the cover loose with the opposite side of the screwdriver.

The cover finally pops open, exposing wires and circuits. She takes off her goggles and points a tiny flashlight that is also part of the electric screwdriver. She then removes her thick gloves by biting on her gloves and pulling her hand away. With her bare hand, she starts pushing off wires with her gloved hand and reaches further in with her bare hand. She feels her fingers going through the still-warm interior of the satellite until she grabs a component and pulls it out with a strong but controlled motion.

The component had a thick carbon and steel casing with extended pins to which the component is connected. Debra takes off her lower mask exposing her red lips. With her warm breath hitting the cold air making fog with every breath, she says

"There you are!"

John comes back to her carrying some charred broken pieces of the satellite asking,

"Find anything?"

She stretches her ungloved hand holding the satellite component up to John saying

"Yeah, baby! Got its imaging storage."

Suddenly, Debra notices a small drone hovering above them while looking up over John's shoulder. She slips the component into her vest pocket and runs towards the snow crawler to grab the binoculars. John, not knowing what's happening says

"Hey! What's going on?"

Debra focuses in on the drone with the binoculars and says

"We are being watched! Look up!"

John drops the debris he was carrying and looked up to see the drone about 100 meters above them.

"It's a medium-range drone! Whoever is watching is not far."

Debra zooms in on the hovering drone and can see its lenses changing direction as the drone tries stabilizing itself in the blowing wind.

"Can't see any markings on it. Whoever it is, must be really interested in the satellite."

John starts fast walking back to the crawler.

"Debra, try taking pictures of it with the binoculars..."

Debra tries to stable herself by leaning on the front part of the crawler to take better images of it.

As soon as she starts taking clear shots of the drone, it suddenly speeds off, as it knew it was being watched.

"It's leaving," Debra says.

John climbs into the driver's side and yells

"Time to go! Get in!"

Debra puts her glove back on and climbs into the crawler. John immediately starts the vehicle and makes a U-turn to start heading back.

John starts switching on other sensors.

"I'm turning on the weapons guidance systems! This area is restricted and no outside drones are allowed within 200 kilometers of our stations."

John flicks a large switch cover upwards to expose his vehicle's main guns. The accumulated snow on the roof of the crawler was pushed aside by two main guns that automatically lifted off its base and pointed rearwards.

John then switches his monitor to target radar tracking.

"Try to contact the Australians on Davies station!"

says John as he brings the snow crawler to full speed following his own tracks.

Debra goes on the communicator to try to contact the Australian base.

Back at the satellite crash site, the silence of the Antarctic winds was suddenly interrupted by roars of two grey and white camouflage thruster-driven transport crafts that started circling the crash site, blowing snow in all directions.

The craft's thrusters would tilt in multiple directions to stabilize the transport. The transports landed on opposite sides of the satellite and soldiers in snow camo face-covered uniforms and weapons streamed out of their lowered cargo bay doors. The soldiers encircled the crash site with military precision. One of the soldiers said on his headset communicator...

"The area is clear sir."

Three figures, two wearing black, and one wearing an expensive-looking grey jacket, all three had face coverings and sunglasses, started walking out of one of the transports. One of the figures in black had a satchel bag and proceeded to the satellite while the other figure would stand close to the satellite.

"Well!?" says the man in grey to the other one going over the satellite. A woman's voice answered

"It's not here. They took it ..."

The man in grey looked up to the blue sky and yelled "Damn it! I knew this would happen!" He looks at one of the soldiers nearest him and says

"Get Burkley out here, now!" The soldier nods and runs towards the second transport. The soldier returns with a man wearing a non-combatant civilian winter outfit. His face was not covered and one of his eyeglasses had a crack. He was shivering from the cold as he was brought to the man in grey.

"If you had not made a mistake in failing to totally destroy the satellite, I wouldn't even have to be here at the bottom of the world!"

The other man in black took one look at the soldier that brought him out of the transport and before the civilian could try to plead for his life, the soldier fired three rapid shots. The shots rang out and echoed in the distance as the civilian fell on the blood-splattered snow facing up as the mist from his breathing slowly lessened with every breath.

"We can still obtain the image component ..."

says the other man in black. The man in grey adjusts his collar to tighten it from the cold

"I don't need to obtain it, I want it destroyed! Something that guy should have done in the first place."

The soldier in black pulls down his mask in frustration showing a neatly trimmed bearded mercenary face.

"Shall I call in the raptors sir?"

The man in grey starts turning around and walks towards the transport followed by the woman with a satchel.

"Do what you must do Colonel. Drop me off first at my ship, and Kim will be with you to make sure you complete your contract."

As transport engines start revving up for take-off, the bearded colonel waves to the soldiers to fall back to their transports. He then turns to the soldier who shot the civilian and orders him to burn the body.

"I don't want the body identified"

Burkley's body was still on fire when the transports started flying off the surface of the deep snow, blowing the black smoke from the burning body mixed with ice spreading on the surface.

John and Debra were about halfway to Station Zebra when John heard a beeping sound from his monitors. He glances at the radar tracking screen and sees two blimps coming from behind them.

"Here they come!" says John while Debra initiates the flare distraction mode.

"Hope your flares aren't jammed because we really need them now!"

Shouts Debra, as she flips the flare switches on Auto mode. A pair of raptor drones, each the size of a small plane, were speeding to within firing range of the snow crawler.

John further increased the speed, making the crawler jump off snow bumps. Debra tightens her seat harness as one of the raptors releases a small missile toward them. The radar tracking started beeping wildly as the screen showed a red dot moving rapidly toward them.

"Incoming!"

yells John, as he waits a few more seconds. He suddenly takes a left and the flare fires automatically, causing a bright light into the windows of the crawler.

The flare shoots out towards the right, making the missile change its course. The missile intercepts the flare about 75 meters above them. The missile explodes violently sending shrapnel hitting the outside of their vehicle.

The auto-tracking main guns on their crawler lifted the snow off the roof, swiveled around, and started firing rapidly at the approaching death drones, hitting the first raptor and tearing its wing off, sending it tumbling down into the icy surface.

John and Debra see the explosion of the downed raptor while the second raptor makes a roaring sound as it passes above them. They could see their gun's tracer bullets shadowing the remaining raptor as it takes a large turn and starts flying in front of them.

The second raptor fires off two missiles as their radar starts alarming again. John can see the two red dots blinking on his screen rapidly closing in on them.

John drives the crawler directly into the path of the missiles in front of them and stumps down on the accelerator.

"What the hell are you doing?" Yells Debra.

Without looking at Debra, John says

"Just be ready to fire off all flares on my signal!"

As the crawler's guns continue to fire rapidly at the incoming raptor, John looks at the radar, does quick mental calculations, and says

"Three, Two, One...all flares now!"

He slams his foot on the brakes plowing the forward portion of the crawler into the snow and lifting the back end of the vehicle at an almost 45-degree angle in the air, sending the flares forward into the incoming heat-seeking missiles.

The rapid guns, making a sweeping motion shred both the raptor and the second missile. The first missile explodes just in front of them as it made contact with the flares. Missile fragments go through their front bulletproof windshields, hitting John on his outer left deltoid, and just missing Debra, hitting the right side of her seat.

The guns were still firing at the crashing raptor as it started descending in front of them.

"C'mon! C'mon!"

shouts John, as the main guns continue firing, trying to knock out the raptor coming towards them. Though the raptor has been effectively neutralized, it was still like a missile flying toward them.

John quickly unbuckles his harness and grabs Debra, pulling her to the space between their seats. He pushes her to the floor of the vehicle as the gliding raptor's wing rips the main guns off the snow crawler, taking the roof off the vehicle. The raptor crashes and explodes about 40 meters behind their now roofless vehicle. They could smell the fumes of the burning raptor as snow gently floated into the vehicle through the exposed ripped open roof.

Debra, still under John's protective arms tries to lift her head. "Are we still alive?"

John looked up to see the jagged metal edges that encircled the opening of their vehicle.

"I think we're still alive"

John kicked Debra's door open and they slowly climb down the crawler. They looked at the raptors burning wreckage and then back at their roofless damaged vehicle.

The crawler's tracks were badly damaged from fragments of the forward missile.

The vehicle had no power as shrapnel ripped through several wirings inside the control panel. Debra walks towards crashed raptor that was still on fire. Its rear side was un-damaged and she started looking at the underside portion of the raptor's tail.

"What are you doing? We have to get going!" Says, John.

She sees a small maintenance door on the rear end of the drone. She reaches for her compact electric screwdriver from her right vest Pocket and opens the small panel to expose a serial number. She turns on her head camera to take a photo of the serial number.

"These numbers can always be traced... This is evidence of whom we are dealing with..."

John grabs two rifles, two backpacks, and two ammo vests from the back side of their wrecked vehicle.

"Debra, we have to get going. Whoever they are, we just brought down two of their multi-million-dollar toys and those things were sent to kill us. So, whatever it is in that memory component, seems to be important enough for them to even come all the way down here to get it."

Debra starts walking back to John, puts on one of the ammo vests, and takes a rifle from John. She looks at her wrist locator.

"There is a crevasse not far from here. Stable enough, but it's a shortcut to my station. This way, we won't expose our heat signatures and we will be under cover most of the time."

John, while checking his rifle says "You sure about that? You know I don't like walking through those things..." Debra smiles and slings her rifle on her shoulder.

"C'mon John, don't be a Sissy...Trust me. Bring ropes, harnesses, crampons, and ice axes."

John grabs some chemical light sticks

"Here, carry some just in case you bring us to a darker side of those crevasses."

John and Debra get to the edge of a crevasse. Debra kneels to take a look down at the dark blue ice opening.

"I'll go first. Make sure our line is secure."

She says as she takes her harness out of her backpack and starts putting it on.

"You sure? You know I can go first you know and..."

"Don't be silly John, you're heavier, so you can support my weight going down."

Debra makes it to the bottom of the crevasse and yells up to John.

"I'm good, you can start coming down now..."

John lowers their rifles tied to a separate line. Debra grabs the rifles and frees them from the line. John, slowly but surely, finally makes it down.

"Seems you haven't forgotten our training yet?"

says Debra while smiling.

"Give me a break, you know I almost failed the course because of my claustrophobia..."

"I thought you took medication for that?"

John frowns and says

"Medication! You cure one illness, and you get sick of another. I think I can handle myself till we get to your station."

Debra gives John a quick kiss on the cheek as John starts tying up the ropes.

"What's that for?" asks John.

"That's for saving my life in the Crawler. I saw how damaged my seat was, I could have been torn apart in that seat..." John puts the ropes around his shoulder.

"Don't mention it. You would have done the same for me."

The two military transports came down on the ice crawler wreck, and the bearded colonel was surveying the damage done to their raptors.

"Can't believe that a single ice crawler could take out two raptors. It's a good thing we dropped him off his ship before coming here. He'll surely want to kill the two raptor drone pilots..."

A soldier comes running from the transport.

"Sir, the drones have followed the snow tracks to a crevasse just north of here."

The colonel kicks the side of the damaged crawler in frustration.

"Let's get there now. Tell Eagle 2 to proceed to the nearest U.S. substation and occupy it. Tell them to jamb all communications in the area. I have a feeling that's where they are going."

John and Debra continue walking the bottom of the crevasse when they hear the large military transport hovering above them. The smooth bluish ice walls that reflected the light from above were suddenly shaking to the loud noise of the carrier's thrusters above. Ice crystals were falling from above and the winds and snow were being blown swirling into the narrow crevasse opening above.

The sound was deafening as the vibrations of the transport would resonate within the ice walls and caves.

"Stand still," says Debra, as the transport's sound slowly starts fading away.

As they continue through the deep icy caves, they started hearing an animal cry. They moved along the icy cavern and chanced upon a white baby bear trapped in a deep narrow slit of ice further below them.

"Look! A baby polar bear!"

"A What?" Debra kneels beside the edge of the narrow slit to take a closer look.

"A polar bear." Says Debra. John took a peek down the hole.

"There are no Polar Bears in Antarctica."

Debra, still on her knees looks up at John and says

"Give me the rope..."

John pulls back and says "No way, we don't have time for this." Debra stands up and grabs the rope around John's shoulder.

"We need all the good Karma we can get right now. First Raptor drones, two at that, trying to turn us into coloring for the snow, now transports with who knows how many bad guys in them after us." She grabs the rope from John and makes a fixed loop at one end. As she tries to lasso the baby bear below and says

"Don't you remember, five years ago, they tried to make an experiment to bring Polar bears here because they were losing their ice homes in the north?"

"Yeah, I remember that. But wasn't that a flop experiment, because the other prey animals would not survive since they were not used to running away from predators, and the bears would easily decimate the seal and penguin populations..."

Debra luckily gets the noose around the shoulders of the baby bear and starts pulling it up.

"That's right! But apparently, they were not able to catch all the bears they brought in because there was a problem with the electronic tags. Apparently, most of the tags were not as waterproof as they were supposed to be."

As Debra starts pulling the animal up, John lays down his rifle and starts helping Debra pull up the crying animal.

"Oh! You're such a cutie aren't you!"

Says Debra as the baby bear starts licking Debra's face.

"Wait till you meet its mother...or its father...Then tell me about

cute..." John says.

Debra starts giggling as she lets the baby bear down.

"Can we go now?"

Debra, still smiling at the cuteness of the baby bear, starts walking. The baby bear almost instinctively starts following Debra.

"Just what we need, another mouth to feed," says John.

They start slowly ascending to the surface as the path they were taking slowly slops out of the crevasse. As they reached the surface, the baby bear at Debra's feet started whining.

"It's probably hungry. God knows how long it's been down there. Got any food in your pack?"

John reaches for the side pocket of his backpack and brings out a thick stick of beef jerky. He takes it out of its wrapper and hands it over to Debra.

"Here you go!" Says Debra as she starts feeding the baby bear. As John turns around to check on his rifle hanging on his shoulder, He freezes.

"Debra...Don't make any sudden moves..."

Debra looks at where John is facing. They both see a huge Polar Bear sniffing the air and looking at them.

"Debra, I want you to meet Mama Bear..."

John slowly grabs more beef jerky from his backpack and starts unwrapping them.

"Is Baby Bear done with his first Jerky?"

Debra slowly stands up and says

"Yes..." John starts tossing pieces of beef jerky toward the direction of Mama Bear. The Baby bear follows the trail of meat on the snow. John says with a soft voice.

"Debra, start moving away slowly. No sudden moves."

They started walking slowly away from the baby bear when suddenly, out of a mound of ice near the sniffing bear, appeared another, bigger bear.

"Looks like Papa Bear decided to crash the party..." says Debra

John threw the remaining beef jerky he had left, and they both started walking a little faster. As they slowly but steadily walked further away from danger, they could see the baby bear being reunited with its family.

"The next time you decide to rescue an animal, make sure it's an animal that isn't able to make us their next meal...ok?"

The two grey and white camouflage military transports landed at Debra's base. The first soldiers out of the transport encircled the small outpost perimeter, while the second set of soldiers went straight for the elevated living quarters.

They rushed up the stairs to the main entrance and placed light charges on the doors. Explosions rang out and the doors were kicked in. The soldiers tossed flash bangs and then rushed inside the entrances of the base. They started going through all of the living and work areas of the base.

Inside one of the transports, the bearded Colonel got a radio call from one of his men.

"All clear sir..."

The Colonel walked out of the carrier. His head swiveled to look around the base. He stops to call one of his men as he sees a transport refueling depot about 50 meters from the main elevated quarters of the base. He calls the nearest soldier.

"Check those depots, see if we can use the fuel for our transports..."

He takes off his snow mask and starts heading towards the nearest breached entrance of the base while his men are on high alert inside the base. He walks towards the base's main communication desk and tells one of his men

"Check the user's log...I want to know when was the last time this base make contact and to whom."

One of the soldiers takes off his goggles and gloves and starts going through the communications log. The colonel continues walking down the other areas of the base.

He enters a room with Debra's pictures with John, framed on Debra's bedside table. He grabs the framed picture and holds it up to his face and reads

"To Debra, Looking forward to another midnight summer. Love, John"

The colonel smiles then smash the picture frame on the corner of the Bedside table, breaking the glass of the picture frame, takes out the photo, then radios

"Kim! Come in here. I've got something for you."

The colonel heads back to the communications room and grabs a seat beside the soldier who was working on the computer log. He stretches his legs and puts his boots up on the work table, scattering snow and mud that was still lodged in the tracks of his boots.

The Colonel could hear quick footsteps and a woman's voice from the next room.

"Where's the Colonel?"

Kim walks into the room, brushing the snow off her shoulders. She removes her headgear and her long black straight shiny hair came flowing out of her headgear

"I hate this cold gear!"

The Colonel smiles at her and kicks a wheeled seat to her.

"I thought you were used to the cold weather...you know ...being from North Korea..."

She takes off her gloves and sits.

"Shut up Colonel! Remember, I don't work for you..."

The Colonel opens his jacket and takes out a silver flask,

"This is my crew, Kim, my men, so this is my party."

He twists open the flask to take a sip of whisky. Kim loosens her collar.

"You didn't ask me to come out of the comfort of your transport for nothing...What do you want?"

The Colonel pulls out the picture of Debra and John and hands it over to Kim.

"I need you to go on your system and see what you can find out about them..."

Kim takes off her gloves and reaches for the picture.

"Lovely couple. Handsome man...you want his number?"

The colonel could hear his men start laughing under their face shields. He takes one look at his men and they suddenly stiffen up and stop laughing. The soldier beside the colonel checking on the communications desk says

"Sir, the last transmission from this base was last night to Zebra station not far from here."

The colonel stands up and goes to a coffee maker in the corner of the room. He checks the pot if it still had coffee in it. Kim puts the photo down on the work desk, stands up, and removes her thick black jacket exposing a pistol in a leather holster shoulder strap on her.

She starts opening some cabinets.

"We might as well make fresh coffee while we are here."

says Kim as she rummages through the cabinets looking for more coffee.

Debra and John had come near the outer perimeter of the base. John was looking through his binoculars and sees the two transports and several soldiers encircling the base.

"Got any ideas?"

Debra, checking on her backpack pockets says

"I know I have it here somewhere..."

"Have what?"

Debra starts opening the rest of the side pockets and brings out a set of access cards.

"There they are!" John Asks

"What are those for?"

Debra points to a thick patch of ice to the left of the base.

"If we could make it to that low Ice wall, we could enter the base by a ground entrance. There is a ground shaft entrance that connects to a tunnel leading to the garage where we could get our hands on some hover cycles."

Debra starts removing her bright red jacket and starts burying it in the snow. Before John could say anything, Debra says

"Don't worry, I always put a set of white thermal camo jackets in the tunnel area."

They both start crawling towards the side of the snow mound embankment that would cover their approach toward the base.

They reach the low-rise snow wall and follow it toward the back of the base. They suddenly hear two guards talking just behind the snow wall they were hiding at.

They could faintly hear the muffled conversation of the two soldiers, and they could smell tobacco burning in the air.

"Cigarette break..."

John whispers to Debra. Not risking a chance for them to be discovered, John and Debra kept still in the snow. Then they hear the soldier's communicators asking them to report to one of the transports.

One of the soldiers responded to the call, while another soldier flicked his cigarette over the snow wall, landing on John's head.

Its embers sparked across John's face as he tried hard not to react. They could hear the two soldiers start walking away toward the base.

"I hate smokers..."

John says as he wipes the ash off his face with fresh snow. They continue their low crawl behind the snow wall.

They reached a white circular metal door embedded just below the snow. Debra starts to shiver as her thermal suit tries its best to keep her warm and wipes the snow off its surface then brings out her access card and swipes it across a sensor next to a red flashing light at the center of the door.

There was a muffled sound of the unlocking mechanism and the flashing red light turned green. The door lifted open and the sound of the hydraulics became louder as the door opening widened.

"Ladies first..."

Debra starts climbing down the chrome-plated ladders at the walls of the tubular shaft. Thin blue LED lights turned on lining the walls of the shaft. John follows down and then presses a large red button at the top of the ladder, automatically closing the door above them.

They reach the bottom of the shaft and cautiously start walking down the underground corridor. Debra pulls her access cards out to open another door.

"What are you doing?" asks John.

The metal door started sliding open and lights started to illuminate the room. There were various small arms to bigger shoulder missile launchers that could take out a large transport.

"Now that's what I'm talking about!"

says John as he grabs one of the launchers off the rack. Debra grabs a white camouflage jacket, extra magazines, grenades, first aid kit, and throws them in her backpack.

John grabs a pair of mini proximity mines and places one in each thigh pocket. As Debra starts walking out of the storage room, John grabs one more proximity mine and flicks a safety switch off, and places it just outside the door area of the cache.

"Leave the door open,"

Says John as they both start walking down the corridor.

Meanwhile, on the surface, a soldier notices crawl marks in the snow. He follows the snow marks to the locked metal ground door. He radios in.

"We have intruder tracks on the north side. Requesting back up..."

Two other soldiers radio in and confirm that they will be in his position.

John and Debra reach the end of the underground corridor and the ladder below the garage area.

They climb the ladder and Debra swipes the door with her access card and the circular door above them unlocks and opens. Debra slowly peeks out the shaft entrance with her pistol.

"It's clear..." She climbs out of the shaft and reaches for the shoulder launcher that John extends up to her.

She removes the covers of the hovercycles. Just as John was about to close the hatch of the ascending tunnel, two soldiers made their way into the underground tunnels and reached the storage room full of arms. A soldier takes another step and the proximity mine beeps, then explodes, blasting a rush of hot air unto John's face as he was closing the hatch. John slams the access door shut and pushes a work trolley, filled with heavy metal parts on top of the hatch.

Debra slings her backpack and rifle and gets on a snow hover. "That one is yours! Let's go!"

John slings his rifle and straps his missile launcher with elastic cords at the compartment area behind his hover seat.

They both flick on their start switches and bluish lights emanated from the underside of their hovers. Their vehicle's engines started whistling like high-pitched turbo jets, and both hovers started lifting off the ground.

Debra presses a button on her control panel and the garage gate started sliding open. The garage area was slowly getting brighter as the large garage doors were opening.

Suddenly they saw two soldiers turn around as they noticed the doors opening. They start walking towards the garage while one of the soldiers had his hand in the air waving to John and Debra not to move. Debra quickly pulls out her sidearm and starts firing at the soldiers. The soldiers instinctively went to kneeling firing positions and started firing back.

Bullets buzzed a few inches from John while others started hitting Debra's front headlights. John lowered his body behind the bulletproof plexy glass front windshield of the snow hover and pressed on the accelerator with his right foot.

The snow hovers blasted out of the garage and John steered directly at the two soldiers. Their rifles fire was bouncing off John's windshield, making large deep scratches as he accelerated toward the two firing soldiers.

Debra quickly followed right behind John. One of the soldiers manage to jump clear of John's throwing the soldier several meters from where he was standing. Debra quickly passed the soldiers just behind John.

As the remaining soldier turned around and started putting Debra on his electronic rifle sights, the soldier says to himself

"I've got you now..."

Suddenly, with a loud angry roar, a large bear grabs the soldier's rifle with her teeth and pounds the soldier to the ground with its large paws.

Debra and John could hear the screaming of the soldier as he was attacked by the bear. They could hear the loud shrieking cries of the soldier being attacked by the huge bear. The perimeter guard's attention was more on helping the soldier being attacked by the bear, making fewer rifles being pointed at them.

John looks back just to check on Debra. She catches up with John and could both see other soldiers firing at them, but they were well out of range for their close-quarters battle sights. They could also see the bear running away from the base with its bloodied mouth and paws making a fading red track in the snow.

Their snow hovers were at full speed, smoothly gliding above a few feet from the snow's surface. Debra signals to John that she wanted to lead the way.

John's hand signals back in agreement as she knew where the dangerous crevasses were hidden.

The Colonel and Kim hear the rifle shots ringing out as radio chatter among the soldiers overlaps one another.

"Captain Stevens! Report! Says the colonel, as he grabs his jacket and gloves off the work table. Kim sits comfortably with her legs crossed at the table and continues to sip coffee off a cup with an American Flag printed on it.

"Trouble Colonel? "

She says softly as the colonel takes a radio report from one of his officers.

"They escaped from the rear..."

The Colonel snaps.

"Destroy the base!"

The other two soldiers follow the colonel as the soldier on the desk started finishing up copying files from the computer.

Kim slowly stands up and starts putting on her black jacket. She grabs her headgear and starts walking out the door. In her hand was the picture of the couple.

The soldier slips a small electronic charge at the data dock and presses Enter. Kim looks back at the room just before the computer gave out a small explosion burning out the communications center. She hung the picture of John and Debra on her red lips as she puts on her gloves. Then she walks out saying

"Time to catch up with John and Debra". She heads outside and puts on her dark sunglasses, seeing the first transport already flying away as the remaining soldiers were running toward the open cargo bay of the second transport.

She was the last to enter the transport as the cargo bay door already started closing with her just a few steps into the transport. The transport lifted making a storm of snow around the base.

It circled around the base, then fired two missiles hitting the elevated living quarters, supply, and garage areas. Bright orange and red fire clouds expanded skyward as black smoke filled the clear blue sky. Kim looked out the window to see an American flag toppled off a broken pole floating gently into the snow like a dead leaf at the start of winter.

John noticed Debra slow down while she was trying to look at her wrist so she could get her bearings.

"Wanna Stop first?" asked John as his snow hover started lowering itself to the surface of the snow. Debra Seeing that John has lowered his hover, slowed down as well. Debra's craft slid into thick snow as its engines came to a stop.

Debra pushes her sleeve up to check her watch on their coordinates. She tries tapping on her wristwatch and lifting it in different directions to see if it is calibrated correctly.

"My GPS signal is weak..." says Debra. John turns off his vehicle, gets off his seat, and starts taking off his headgear.

"It must be the shallow sun's rays on the horizon. Sometimes it has an effect on GPS readings..."

Debra Steps off her vehicle and lifts her hover seat to open a compartment. She pulls out a work pad and takes off her right-hand glove. She starts swiping the work pad to see if the GPS signal on the pad has better reception. A map display was generated on the pad showing her pre-marked indicators of hidden crevasses.

She turns and looks in one direction and says

"That way. There is a shallow crevasse not far from here where we can take a rest and recharge the hover batteries."

John takes out his binoculars and looks in the direction that Debra pointed out.

"Shallow enough to hide the snow hovers?"

Debra starts packing her work pad and puts her glove back on.

"Yup! Won't need ropes this time. Those Military transports may be slow, but they can still catch up to us. I'm pretty sure they will head to Zebra Base. We won't have time to call the Aussies for backup at Davies Point before they get to us at Zebra base."

John looks at his watch and says:

"You suggesting we let them bypass us before going to Zebra?" Debra turns around to John,

"I'm saying that we rest first, charge our batteries, and head for the nearest Davies Point substation."

"But what about Zebra? They'll get there and mess up my place!" Says John. Debra walks towards John while taking off her goggles

"John, you know very well we don't stand a chance against Two soldier-filled transports, who knows where those mercs are from? They seem desperate enough to attack US Substations…"

John looks up at the clear blue sky and lets out a large deep breath in frustration.

"C'mon John, it's almost one in the morning, we need rest. We don't want to get Winter-over syndrome, do we?"

John gets on his snow hover and starts up his engine. A whirling high pitched turbo sound started shaking the snow near Debra's feet.

"Lead the Way then…" John says. Debra puts the work pad back under her seat and starts her engine.

They reach the entrance of the shallow crevasses and lowered their snow vehicles' throttles just enough to keep the hovers above the snow. They both slowly guide their vehicles down the shallow crevasse. Debra looks around the smooth shiny blue ice cave walls.

"This spot is good." As she switches off her vehicle and unties the bungee cords just behind her seat. She takes out a rolled-up solar panel and attaches a wire to the snow hover. She starts walking out of the crevasse.

"Your solar panel is just behind your seat, John,"

Debra says as she exits the entrance of the crevasse. She looks at her long shadow to see where the sun is shining, places the now extended rolled-out solar panel, and angles it to face the sun. John follows outside and places his solar panel beside hers on the snow. Debra looks at the horizon as John stands beside her.

"It's one of the few things with color around here, and one of the few places where the sunrise looks exactly as the sunset…if ever…"

John takes Debra's hand and they as they walk back to the dark blue interior of the ice. They pop out a small black opaque tent that keeps any light from entering the tent. They cuddle one another as they both fall asleep, warm in each other's arms.

Six hours later, John wakes up and slowly makes his way out of their tiny black tent, being careful not to wake Debra. He walks towards the opening of the crevasse and sees the sun has moved to another spot on the horizon. He then turns towards the solar panels and disconnects the wires plugged into the panels. He starts rolling them one at a time and then sees Debra coming out of the crevasse entrance.

"Has it been six hours already?"

Debbie asks as she starts walking towards John. He starts rolling the power lines around the Rolled-up solar panels and says

"It's really hard to tell unless you remember where the sun was at the horizon..."

He hands Debra a rolled-up solar panel and starts rolling up the second power cord.

"We best get going...The outer Australian bases should just be a few hours from here."

They both head back into the crevasse to pack up their tent and stow away their solar panels back behind their snow hover seats. John ties down his rifle above the compartment area behind his seat and slings the compact missile launcher around his shoulder. Debra switches on her snow hover's engine and her power indicator at 96 percent charged.

"Those solar panels really do work. That's why I like Norwegian Technology, not cheap, but dependable."

John starts his hover and puts his headgear on. Before he straps on his snow mask, he says

"Keep trying to contact Davies Station, with any luck, we could call them for backup."

Debra gives John a Thumbs up and accelerates her hover vehicle out of the crevasse. John follows and soon they are at full speed again hovering on top of the snow.

Back at Zebra station, the mercenary soldiers at the perimeter of the station were starting to feel the effects of prolonged sunlight and lack of sleep. Some of them would occasionally dose off while standing, and then suddenly wake themselves up as they lose their own balance standing in the snow.

One of the soldiers would go around, making sure they would inhale from a mouthpiece connected to an aerosol can provided to each soldier, strapped on their ammo vests.

The soldiers inhaled from these cans during extended missions that required them to stay awake.

Some of the soldiers were on top of the roofs of the carriers removing the snow build-up on the top of the carriers, and clearing the large air vents of the large turbine engines.

Inside the Station, Kim has made herself at home inside John's room having taken a shower and resting on his bed wearing only her black underwear. She would look at John's picture and smell his pillows, imagining she was his lover.

In the communications room, one of the soldiers picks up a signal from one of the drones.

"Sir, we have movement..."

The Colonel, seated on another work chair in the room, deeply inhales from a mouthpiece connected to a canister and says

"Show me!"

The soldier opens up a window on the large glass monitor in front of them showing a live feed from one of the drone's cameras. It showed John and Debra speeding across the snow on a thermal image of green and white.

"Sir, the drone indicates they are not moving in this direction."

The colonel stands up and says

"Fire up carrier one. Give them coordinates and directions. Tell them to go ahead. We will follow on carrier two."

The colonel walks towards John's sleeping quarters and enters the darkened room. Kim's clothes `were neatly hanging on the backrest of the chair in front of a small work table.

The colonel could see steam from the dim light coming from the slightly opened bathroom door where Kim had just helped herself to a warm shower.

He sees Kim comfortably between the sheets and hugging a pillow between her legs.

"Wanna join me?

She says with her long black hair spread across her face only showing one eye and her red lips. She slowly pulls down the sheets exposing her body to the colonel. The colonel takes a quick look at his watch

"I think we have a little time..."

The Colonel locks the door behind him and walks to Kim on the bed.

John and Debra were speeding above the snow when John notices the drone watching them from above at his five o'clock.

"We have been spotted!"

Debra looks back at John as he points up to the sky. Not far ahead of them was a large cluster of exposed rock formations.

"If we could reach those rocks up ahead, we will be within radio range of the Australian outpost."

As they were about two kilometers from the large rock formation, The military transport was now behind them, bullets blasting the snow beside their vehicles, trying to hit them from the air with their forward guns. John and Debra started swerving their hovers to give the carrier harder targets to hit.

"Let's separate!"

shouts John, as he suddenly makes a hard turn to the right.

The carrier pilot tells the forward gunner to stay on Debra's hover. The automatic fire was getting uncomfortably closer to Debra's hover as a single round hits her hover rear compartment seat.

Black smoke starts streaming from her vehicle and warning alarms start flashing in her front console as she pushes the hover to its maximum speed while trying to zigzag across the snow.

John circles back and finds himself below the rear end of the carrier. The carriers tail guns open fire at John as he keeps his vehicle going from side to side behind the carrier, making it difficult for the carrier's rear gunner to close in on his target.

John presses the autopilot button and slings his rifle to fire at one of the carrier's thrusters. His shoulder is ponded by his rifle's full auto firing at the carrier.

The skin on the carrier's thrusters starts peeling metal pieces bursting away from the craft with every bullet hit. The carrier's rear gunner takes careful aim and hits John's vehicle on its front end, sending the snow hover crashing nose first into the snow, tossing John several meters in front of his vehicle.

He wildly tumbles into the snow and his hover starts spewing out a dark heavy cloud of black smoke. Debra sees the black smoke in her rearview mirror and takes a steep left turn.

The carrier Pilot follows Debra as she doubles back to John's position. John picks himself up off the heavy snow and sees Debra making a left turn circling back towards him.

"What are you doing Debra?"

He asks himself, as he staggers back to his crashed vehicle. Debra's vehicle started spewing more smoke from its hit rear area as the pilot gained confidence and starts lowering the height of the carrier.

"We need her alive. Colonel's orders."

Says the pilot, as the front gunner relaxes but keeps Debra in his sights. The raising smoke from Debra's snow hover starts to blur the view of the Pilot's front windshields.

The Pilot sees Debra's vehicle starts slowing down as she gets closer to John's smoking-wrecked vehicle.

"Where's the other one?"

Asks the front gunner as his view is fully engulfed by the heavy black smoke from Johns's burning vehicle. The Pilot puts the carrier to hover, as heavy smoke keeps them from seeing out their windows.

The smoke clears for a second when a sudden gust of wind disturbs the smoke in front of the carrier. John fires his shoulder-mounted rocket at the cockpit of the carrier.

The pilot sees the rocket being fired and attempts to fly the carrier away from the missile's path. The carrier's engines were on full thrust as the carrier gets hit just below the cockpit area, killing the front gunner instantly. The carrier spins out of control as the soldiers inside the carrier brace to the walls of the craft, and weapons accidentally go off inside the craft killing more soldiers. The carrier flips to its side, crashed, and broke in two, spilling out men and materials from its interior to the snow when it crashed into flames with a huge explosion of fiery red, orange and black mushroom cloud about fifty meters from where John and Debra were standing.

The reflection of the fire and explosions from the crash was visibly clear on Debra's snow goggles, as she slowly removes them and makes them rest around her neck.

"You don't see that every day..."

She says, as she slowly walks up to John who is now flat on his back, breathing heavily, with the launcher just beside him. She gets down on one knee to pull John up by his ammo vest. John starts grunting in pain.

"Slowly! God, that hurts..."

"That's just your stiff muscles talking...C'mon! Stand up..."

Debra manages to get John on his feet. She then walks towards John's still-burning snow hover.

She starts throwing snow on the hover to extinguish the remaining fire while John starts limping toward Debra's hover. He sits down on the rear seat and reaches down to grab a handful of snow to stop the smoke that is burning through the seat.

He then grabs a canister of water strapped on the side panel of the hover and starts drinking.

"How far are we from the nearest Davies outpost?"

"Not far, we can get radio reception if we could get in the middle of those rock formations."

"How soon can the Aussies come to get us?"

"About twenty-five, thirty minutes..."

John takes a look at the rock formation just before them.

Its dark brown weathering color granitoid rocks were formed from ancient volcanic magma solidified to make new rocks like granite, charnockite, and syenite.

The rocks had jagged peaks jutting out like giant fingers reaching out from under the snow. Debra sees John staring at the rocks.

"Sometimes the winds make funny noises in the rocks, something like the sound you hear on solid ice shelves, but different."

As she continues to check John's vehicle for salvageable items.

"I've heard those ghostly snow sounds before..."

Debra collects the remaining rifle magazines from John's snow hover and pushes them into her ammo vest.

"Those rocks are different. The wind bouncing off those rocks makes you feel like someone is always trying to tell you something, especially if you haven't had any sleep..."

John checks his pistol and makes sure he has a round chambered. He then unties the rifle strapped down on Debra's back seat and lightly hits it with his palm to clear the snow off the rifle parts.

Debra slings the rifle on her back and put her goggles back on as she gets into the snow hover where John has already positioned himself to ride behind her.

They pass the smoldering wreck of the downed carrier that has blackened and disturbed a large area of snow with pieces of debris and burnt metal parts scattered in a large area around the crash site. They could distinctly smell the burnt flesh, mixed with metal, artificial plastic, and rubber, which is easy to pick up in the clear Antarctic air.

With their damaged hover, John and Debra reached the edge of the rock formation. They carefully hide their damaged vehicle between smaller rocks and snow. Debra looks at the higher formation of the jagged rocks that are reaching for the clear blue sky.

"There!"

Debra points to one of the higher peaks.

"I'm sure we could get a signal to the Aussies from that peak." John adjusts his thick collar and zips up his outer snow jacket.

"We won't have any protection from the weather up there, but at least, these rocks will keep them from using their Flir system. The rocks are too thick and dense for their infrared systems to detect us."

They start trekking their way up the peak using narrow corridors of the rock formation. They both start to hear the winds vibrating through the rocks and ice making sounds that eerily echo between the rocks. The rocks formed like a giant maze as they would climb slowly toward the peak.

"You sure we are in the right direction?"

asks John, as he suddenly slips and loses his footing on a ledge, pushing smaller rocks and crashing down the narrow spaces between the larger rocks, making high-pitched breaking sounds that echoed out in all directions.

Debra looks back to see John clumsily climbing the rocks below and trying to get a firm footing before pushing himself up the ledge he was hanging on to.

"You O.K.? Need any help?"

John looked up at Debra and waves his hand

"I'm fine. Go ahead. I'll catch up."

As the downed transport carrier was burning, there was a thumping sound from inside the front portion of the wreckage.

A small emergency hatch was kicked open, and out crawled the pilot of the carrier coughing from inhaled smoke in the burning wreck.

His nose and lips were bloodied as he slowly took off his pilot's helmet. He squints and puts his arm up to shield his face from the intense heat of the burning carrier.

He starts limping across the snow looking around for survivors. He sees the bodies of his men thrown out of the broken fuselage, lifeless. Some bodies were still smoking and the captain could not look into the faces of his men. As he was rummaging around for whatever he needed to survive. He then hears the sound of the second carrier coming in. He drops the items in his hands, gets to his feet, and starts waving at the incoming carrier.

The transport takes one circle around the wreck and starts landing in front of him. Its main bay door opens and out comes Kim, stepping off the bay door platform, walks towards the pilot.

The Pilot starts yelling, trying to be heard through the sound of the carrier's engines.

"Where's the Colonel? we need to check if there are any more survivors...Where's the rest of the crew?"

With the carrier's engine sounds drowning out the pilot's words, and the snow storming from the thrusters, the pilot looks over Kim's shoulder to see the Colonel just standing outside the open bay doors. He notices the colonel just staring at him.

The pilot then looks back at Kim to see her pointing a pistol at him.

"I had a feeling it would come to this. The things we do for money...."

Kim fires two quick successive shots into the pilot's chest and is thrown down on the snow. Without saying a word, Kim opens her jacket and slips her pistol into her red leather holster. She turns around and starts walking back to the carrier.

Walks past the colonel.

"You didn't have to do that that you know..."

says the colonel. Kim removes her snow mask and answers

"I know, but sometimes It's better if I do your job for you."

Kim turns and continues further back into the carrier. Two soldiers near the Colonel looked at each other while the colonel could hear one of them saying to the another...

"Cold-hearted North Korean bitch!"

The Colonel pretended not to hear his men's conversation as he slams a button and the bay doors start closing up. The carrier starts lifting off and the blown snow from the carrier's thrusters starts covering the pilot's motionless body. The carrier lifted in a circular flight and started heading toward the rock formation.

Debra had set up a portable antenna she had taken from John's destroyed hover. She connects it to her portable radio receiver and starts trying to make contact with the outer bases of the Australian Davies Station.

John studies the terrain and narrow rock corridors and searches for possible escape routes just in case whoever is after them decides to drop enemy combatants around their area.

"They will have to drop them at this clearing..."

John points to Debra an open space not far from where they set up communications.

"If they try an assault, this area could be a kill box." Debra finally gets through to an Australian base.

"They have locked on their signal and will send a rescue team." John starts counting the remaining rifle magazines they have left and remembers he still has two more anti-personnel proximity mines in his leg pockets. He goes out placing the mines on two pathways to the open ridge.

"Tell the Aussies Not to let their personnel come in on the eastern side." Debra radios back and gives them the instruction.

"What's their ETA?

"They say 25 minutes at the least."

John starts double-checking the rifles and switches the rifle's auto fire rate to semi-auto for single-shot fire. Debra starts putting away her radio set up and remembers she still had two hand grenades she took from her base.

She grabs her backpack and reaches in. She pulls out both grenades and smiles at John

"We still have these!" John smiles back and says

"There's nothing like a red-blooded American female marine! You got some wires in your pack?"

Debra hastily reaches for her backpack once again and brings out a roll of fishing line.

"That will do just fine."

John chooses the third pathway from the rocks to their area and places a trip wire for the first grenade.

"We've covered most of the entry points from the east and part of the north. So, all we have to do is cover southwest."

John grabs his empty backpack and puts a flat heavy stone inside it.

"What is that for?" asks Debra.

"Bait..."

He goes to the center of the rock opening and removes the pin from the remaining grenade and gently places the rock-filled backpack on the grenade's release handle.

"Let's just hope they don't hover above near enough to lift the backpack off the ground."

John and Debra find a spot, protected by large rocks, with a commanding view of the kill box. John lays down his rifle to open his jacket to inspect his shoulder wound. Debra kneels beside him, helping with his thick camo jacket. John lets her inspect his wounds and starts grunting while she tears part of his inside shirt away from his wounds.

"We have to clean it."

Debra reaches for the first aid kit in her thigh pocket. She opens the bright orange plastic kit and brings out a small disinfecting spray can. She starts spraying on John's open wound and a white bubbly foam forms immediately over the wound.

She then tears out a round medical patch from its cover and firmly places it on top of the shoulder wound. John tries his best not to react to the pain, but Debra can see his reaction from the corner of her eye.

"Don't be a sissy marine! You've had worse than this."

She then brings out a tiny syringe and pulls the plastic needle cover off with her teeth. John looks away not wanting to watch the needle go through his skin.

"I remember Borneo. We were sent there to rescue a group of American students kidnapped from the Island of Jolo. Those brats never listen to our embassy's list of hotspots. They think that part of the world is a tropical paradise."

Debra pulls out the syringe and puts it back in the orange first aid kit. John looks at Debra and says

"You were part of that team?"

"Yup, hand-picked me because I spoke a little Filipino, and I volunteered to make sure the Chinese would not re-establish their man-made islands in the West Philippine Sea. You know, the ones we bombed out when they attacked one of our ships?"

"Yeah! I remember that. I thought a major war was coming..."

Debra starts packing the first aid kit and says

"Turns out, the Chinese didn't think their small bases were worth the destruction of their whole country. They figured they had a lot more to lose if total war broke out."

John looks at his shoulder and adjusts his jacket

"So, what happened in Borneo?"

Debra sat down beside him and took a deep breath.

"Our rescue mission at first was ok. We were able to get near the rebel base where they held the 18 American hostages. Most of the guards gave up without a fight.

We took out about another four on our way out of the jungle. We were about five hundred meters from our extraction point when we were surprised by another group.

It was dark and raining. You couldn't see more than a few meters in the thick jungle. I gave the order for some of the men to flank the enemy position.

Continuous fire erupted when the unit was in position. The firing suddenly stopped. I radioed my sergeant to report.

They radioed in telling me to come to their position. I instructed the rest of the men to bring the hostages to the extraction point and I headed back to the flanking force.

As I made my way through the thick jungle and deep mud, I came upon a small trail between tall thick jungle grass with one of my men kneeling, protecting the rear of the flanking force. I asked the private where the rest of the team were, expressionless, through his camouflaged painted face with water dripping down his jungle hat, he pointed towards his rear. I started to hear the cries of women through the roaring sound of the jungle rain.

The men were standing still around the bodies of young boys, five of them, with two women crying and hugging the bloodied bodies of the lifeless boys.

All I could hear was the cries of those mothers, wailing in grief, through the pounding sound of the rain and thunder. I could see the pools of blood mixed with the mud whenever the lightning flashed, showing the grief of a mother's loss, like pictures being taken at a crime scene in a dark place.

The thunder continued to drown out the women's cries as they hugged the bloodied bodies of the young boys. One of the men noticed that two boys were still breathing, So I radioed in command for additional extraction to save the boys. Command gave me a negative, and my sergeant had to pull me out of the area to the waiting carriers."

John looks at Debra and says

"That's tough. So, I guess you had a big fight with your C.O. when you got back..."

Debra stands up to stretch her legs and says:

"Didn't say a word. Walked right up to him at the base and punched him in front of the staff. I took out some of his front teeth."

"Wow!"

"Yup. Threw me in the Brig. Then they started coming out with other charges. The charges didn't stick but I was demoted, then transferred.

I had other operations after. More rescue missions in places you wouldn't think you would have to rescue citizens from.

My last C.O. gave me a choice between a shitty rescue center in Pakistan near the Afghan border or just spending a few months watching over some military outpost at the bottom of the world. They never thought I would pick this place...I needed some time alone..."

"Alone my ass! Took you less than a week to contact me from your base..."

"So, what's your story? Punched your CO or just Slept with a General's daughter?"

John stands up to stretch his legs as well.

"I thought we agreed you wouldn't ask..."

"That's right!" snaps Debra "But now that I've spilled my guts to you, it's your turn."

Suddenly, they hear the familiar sound of the Carrier engines getting louder.

"Looks like my story has to wait."

They both chambered their rifles and start walking to their positions behind rocks.

The Carrier starts making a wide circle around the rock formation. The Pilot of the Carrier sees the clearing where John predicted they would land their carrier.

John sees the carrier start making an approach to the area he knew they would make a landing. The dust from the rocks was flying in all directions as the carrier made its slow approach to the clearing. The soldiers disembarked, rushing out in single file, and fanned out towards the maze of rocks.

John pulls an energy bar from his arm pocket and starts chewing down as Debra takes a sip of water from her canister. They kept their rifles aimed toward the southwest.

The soldiers were grouped in fours, making their way through the rocks. The winds were picking up and the sleepless soldiers were starting to hallucinate, hearing the strange sounds the air made on the rocks, seeing shadows, and trying hard to focus.

John and Debra hear the first explosion that echoes through the rocks from the proximity mine tripped by some of the soldiers, followed by screams of pain and cries for help.

John was about to take his last bite from his energy bar when a second explosion went off. John knew from its distinct sound that the enemy has tripped the wired grenade. The sound was higher pitched compared to the proximity mine. Again, they started to hear screams for help and pain.

Debra takes a look at John as he put out two fingers and smiles at Debra. She smiles back at John then suddenly sees a figure moving at the corner of her eye.

She swings her rifle toward the moving object and sees two soldiers running across the open area. John starts firing at the running soldier as Debra sees another soldier peeking out of the rocks looking for them.

She takes a deep breath to steady her aim and times her trigger pull to the movement of the bobbing target. She pulls the trigger and the rifle kicks her shoulder. She sees the blood splatter from the soldier's head onto the rocks behind him as the soldier's hand and rifle dangle lifelessly to the side of the rocks.

She hears another shot and turns her rifle to the right only to see the dead body of the second soldier in the open taken out by John.

Then they start hearing automatic gunfire coming from another direction. The sounds of the rifles were distinctively different, even the rate of fire sounded different.

"It's the Aussies! They finally made it!"

Debra gave out a breath of relief. Several Australian Army guards have surrounded the carrier.

The continuous sound of the winds in the rocks and the carrier's engines have concealed the approach of the Australian Snow Speeders.

As instructed, they came in on the southwest of the rock formation. The Australians knew these rock formations well, for they would occasionally do some exercises in the rock formation.

John and Debra could faintly hear the commands shouted out by the Australians.

"Sounds like the Aussies are winning..."

A third Explosion disturbed the sound of gun fires in the distance. "I Hope none of the Aussies walked into the last proximity mine,"

says John as he starts to pick up his backpack. Debra also starts grabbing her gear and walks towards John. They head towards the clearing not far from the backpack bait was laid on the ground.

Suddenly, shots rang out and John fell to the ground. Before Debra could get her rifle slung behind her, a woman's voice yelled out from the rock edges. It was Kim with another soldier.

Kim's right ear was bleeding and the right side of her face had been darkened by a blast. Her black jacket was torn on one side with parts of her shoulder exposing her bloodied arm.

The soldier beside her had shattered snow goggles but looked unscathed from the proximity mine, and had his rifle pointed at Debra.

"Where is it?"

"Where's what?"

Kim pulls out her pistol and shoots Debra in the leg. She falls down on the lightly snow-covered rocks.

"Toss the rifle...Slowly!"

In Pain, Debra slowly throws her rifle away.

"Again...Where is it? Or the next bullet will be on your boyfriend's head..."

Kim points her pistol at John's head.

Ok! Ok! ...There...it's in the backpack."

Debra points to the backpack on the ground. Kim Signals to the soldier, and he starts walking toward the backpack. Debra tries to crawl closer to John whose wound was on the side of his midsection. Kim points her pistol back to Debra.

Debra sees the soldier pick up the backpack and hears the clicking sound of its safety handle coming off. Debra covers John with her body as the grenade explodes, Throwing Kim off her feet. Debra tries to reach for John's rifle but Kim quickly gets back on her feet and pulls Debra away from John, pointing her pistol at Debra's head.

"You have no idea what I will do to your boyfriend!"

Debra closes her eyes as Kim slowly points her pistol at Debra's temple. She hears the sound of the winds howling through the rocks and snow.

Its howling winds sang, as it started to relax Debra, as the thought of forgiving herself for her sins in Borneo came flashing into her mind.

She started to see and hear the young boys laughing and playing in a green garden, smiling at her, and telling her everything is OK.

With her eyes closed, she smiles, and her breathing slowed down. Kim's eyes widened with surprise, as she sees the smile on Debra's face.

She was not used to killing anyone with a smile on their face. Kim, angry with what she sees, expresses her bitterness in her eyes.

"Time to Die…"

A Shot rang out, but not from Kim's pistol. Debra opens her eyes to see Kim, still staring at her, but with a bullet hole right between her eyes.

It seemed like an eternity to Debra as Kim's body slowly fell to the ground in front of her. She heard footsteps coming from behind her. She turns to see the pilot of the downed carrier with his pistol and hands in the air.

A few seconds later, the Aussies came to the clearing shouting at the pilot to toss his sidearm and get on his knees. He survived Kim's execution by wearing his bulletproof vest under his uniform.

Two Aussies ran to the pilot to secure him and another two rushed to John and Debra. The Aussie nearest to them radios for stretchers and asks them if there are any other enemy combatants left.

Debra, exhausted from what just happened, just signals to the Aussies. John says

"I think you got the last of them."

Debra pulls out the satellite imaging storage component and hands it to one of the Australian officers.

"This is your Area. I believe this is what they were looking for."

The Officer takes out a plastic bag, and wraps the component carefully.

The Australians carry both John and Debra on stretchers. They pass the bullet-riddled carrier with a few prisoners sitting on the snow. They see the bearded colonel, handcuffed to another prisoner being interrogated by the Australians.

The carrier pilot soon joins the rest of the prisoners and the colonel was surprised to see the pilot still alive. They stared at each other and the colonel, with shame, looked away.

Approaching Sidney harbor, the large luxury yacht of the rich weapons dealer who had hired Kim and the Colonel was sunbathing under the sun beside a pool on the second level, with two sexy women in swimsuits wading while sipping ice tea from tall glasses. His sunglasses reflected the two frolicking women as he took a puff out of his expensive Cuban cigar.

Suddenly, two military crafts came down from the sky and circled the yacht. One of the crafts hovered in front of the speeding yacht and fired warning shots, splashing water high enough to reach the yacht's bridge, forcing the crew to put the ship to a full stop. The winds from the thrusters started blowing hard down on the yacht and made waves, disturbing the calm waters of the bay.

The second craft hovered above the open area where the arms dealer was, now on his feet and shouting to his crew. His bodyguards lower their weapons on the deck and raise their arms as a bay door opens above them and soldiers, all masked, start floating down on their individual jet packs. They scatter throughout the yacht as the two girls get out of the pool and grab their white thick robes.

The Arms dealer smiles while two soldiers approach him. The first one forces him onto the deck as his sunglasses fall into the pool. The second soldier points his rifle to his head. The two women are brought down to another part of the yacht, while a third soldier presses a button on his helmet and starts transmitting.

In an undisclosed location, there were several officers in front of a large monitor. Watching the monitor was a Russian general and his aid, and a high-ranking Chinese Diplomat flanked by his intelligence officers. They see the live feed on the screen being fed by the soldier on the yacht. They see the arms dealer on the ground while a soldier takes a blood sample.

A portable DNA scanner is brought out and the blood is inserted into the side of the scanner. The scanner's monitor reads out the DNA and, in a few seconds, shows the word "Positive ID" and the picture and name of the Arms dealer is shown on the scanner's monitor.

One of the Sitting officers says...

"It's a Positive ID Sir"

Another officer in the room looks at the Russian general and prints out the positive ID of their target.

The soldier on the yacht says

"Ghost One, Waiting for Confirmation to complete the mission"

The Russian and Chinese officials look and nod in agreement.

The officers in the room transmit their commands.

"Ghost One, you are green to complete the mission."

The soldier pushes down the arms dealer to the deck.

"I have Money! Lots of Money! I can make you a rich man!"

Before the arms dealer could say another word, a bullet goes through his head, and blood quickly flows on the expensive yacht's shiny surface and onto the swimming pool

"Not this time..." Says Ghost One.

The transmission is terminated and the Russian and Chinese officials stand up and shake hands, giving a light smile to each other.

A month later, Debra, wearing a sexy two-piece lime green bikini and thick dark sunglasses was comfortably baking in the tropical sun beside an infinity pool overlooking the South China Sea.

John's hand brushes over her shoulders. She gently grabs his hand and brings them slowly to her sun-red kissed lips. He hands her a tropical fruit punch with a tiny parasol and a pineapple slice hanging on the lip of the tall glass with a cherry on top. She draws the straw to her lips and takes a deep refreshing sip.

"Now, this is the life..." she softly says with a smile.

John smiles and says "I think we've earned it. We just stop Russia and China from cutting each other's throats."

"Yeah...I'm sure that's the end of that."

Just when both of them were about to dose off under the sun and soft sounds of the beach waves...a burst of machine gun fire and the sound of people screaming. They both take off their sunglasses and John says

"Here we go again!

The End

9 798215 732342